A Little House in a Big Place

To Dad and Mom, for always building and igniting, homes and creative fire — A.A.

To my father, and to Peter — V.L.

Text © 2019 Alison Acheson

Illustrations © 2019 Valériane Leblond

Kids Can Press gratefully acknowledges the financial support of the Government of Ontario, through the Ontario Media Development Corporation; the Ontario Arts Council; the Canada Council for the Arts; and the Government of Canada for our publishing activity.

Published in Canada and the U.S. by Kids Can Press Ltd.

25 Dockside Drive, Toronto, ON M5A 0B5

Kids Can Press is a Corus Entertainment Inc. company

www.kidscanpress.com

The artwork in this book was rendered in gouache, oil pastels and colored pencils.

The text is set in pencilPete.

Edited by Yasemin Uçar
Designed by Julia Naimska

Printed and bound in Malaysia in 10/2018 by Tien Wah Press (Pte.) Ltd.

CM 19 0 9 8 7 6 5 4 3 2 1

Library and Archives Canada Cataloguing in Publication

Acheson, Alison, 1964-, author

    A little house in a big place / Alison Acheson ; illustrated by Valériane Leblond.

ISBN 978-1-77138-912-9 (hardcover)

    I. Leblond, Valériane, 1985-, illustrator II. Title.

PS8551.C32 L58 2019   jC813'.54   C2018-902055-5

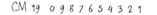

A Little House
in a Big Place

Written by
Alison Acheson

Illustrated by
Valériane Leblond

KIDS CAN PRESS

A girl lived in a little house
in a little town
in the middle of a big place.
Clickety-clack tracks crossed the field behind.

She stood at her window and waved
to the train engineer who passed every day
and she wondered.
About where he came from and where he went.
And if she might go away, too, someday.

The train engineer drove east through the night
and west as the sun came up.
He drove past many towns, but in this one town
a little girl waved to him from a house
with shining colored lights.

His train came over the horizon every morning.
One moment there was only sky, and the next moment
there would be a dot
        that got bigger
                and bigger
                    and bigger

and the dot would become the train.

Every morning the girl waved
and the engineer waved back.

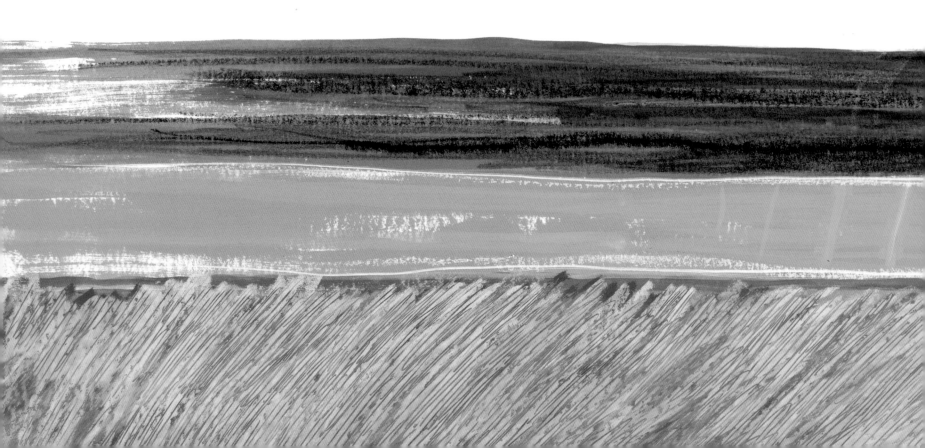

The train rushed and rumbled to the other side of her window
and away
and became a **dot**
a smaller **dot**
an almost invisible dot.

But his wave and her wave together made a home in her heart.

She wondered about the engineer, riding high in the front.
She wondered if he liked his uniform and his engineer's cap.
Maybe he wanted to wear a cowboy hat or a suit
with tails and a top hat.

She didn't know his name and he couldn't know hers.

She didn't know that this day would be his last day driving that train.

The girl stood at her window as she did every morning —
only this time, she saw something sail from the engineer's hand.
She ran out from the little house, but whatever it was —
the sailing something — she couldn't spot.

Instead, she found wild strawberries, hidden and sweet,
and wildflowers along the tracks.
She picked some and lay in the warm-smelling prairie grass,
looked up at the sky,
listened to the songs of the grasshoppers' chirps,
and felt the whoosh of the wind.

The wind whispered, *What is it?*

The girl stood and let the wind push gently at her back;
she let it blow and carry her farther from her little house.

She could see the tiniest speck, a dot
that grew
and grew
and turned out to be ...

... the engineer's cap!
She put it on, and it fit.
Almost.

The train still came over the horizon every morning
with a different engineer.
But the girl didn't always wait by the window.

Sometimes she painted pictures,

sometimes she danced

and sometimes she made up songs
to play on the guitar.

The girl grew up.
She left the little house,
she left the little town,
and she rode a train east —

east to where the sun rises —
disappearing into a small dot
on the edge of the big sky ...

... but ending up somewhere.